# CAPILONGO

TAHIR SHAH

BEATA BANACH

# CAPILONGO

*A Teaching Story*

TAHIR SHAH

BEATA BANACH

MMXXIV

Secretum Mundi Publishing Ltd
124 City Road
London
EC1V 2NX
United Kingdom

www.secretum-mundi.com
info@secretum-mundi.com

First published by Secretum Mundi Publishing Ltd, 2024
A version of this story originally appeared in *Scorpion Soup* by Tahir Shah, 2013

CAPILONGO



Artwork drawn by Beata Banach



A CIP catalogue record for this title is available from the British Library.

ISBN 978-1-915876-04-1

VERSION 05012024

Visit the author's website:
Tahirshah.com

Descend through the layers of an onion and,
as you weep, you will find true wisdom.

*Afghan saying*

# Teaching Stories

When I was small, I was told stories from morning till night.

I was told stories about genies and witches and about great birds that could carry away elephants on their wings... and stories about distant kingdoms and magical lands ruled by warrior kings.

I was told stories of good and bad... stories of hope and others of despair.

I was even told stories about stories.

And all the while, I listened, amazed.

The more I listened, the more my mind worked... and the more I came to understand that these stories had a power about them, a secret lifeblood all of their own.

They were magical instruments, machineries that could alter states of mind and change the way we think.

But most importantly of all, stories can teach us, without us realizing that they are doing so at all.

Part of the default programming of man, stories are within us all.

Born into us, they make us who we are – they make us human.

Since earliest childhood, I have feasted on stories as a way of learning about the world, and learning about myself. They have been my dictionary and my encyclopaedia, my classroom, my guide, and my very best friend.

To descend down through the layers of stories is to be reborn, into a dominion of fantasy – one touched by real magic.

Pre-eminent within the great treasuries of tales, it is teaching stories like this one that have shown me the path to follow beyond the next horizon, and have made me the man I am.

Tahir Shah

In line with his own tradition, a celebrated French writer journeyed to Toledo so that his latest manuscript could be bound in leather by my master, Señor Fernandez, the greatest bookbinder to have ever lived.

Once word of the author's arrival had been received, we all began to prepare.

For days, the apprentices polished and cleaned the workshop, laying out the finest leathers and samples of the most exquisite work.

On the morning that the writer was due to arrive, there was an enormous sense of expectation. Each one of us dressed in our best clothes, polished our shoes until they shone like silver, and greased back our hair with lavender pomade.

At a little after the strike of ten, a magnificent lacquered carriage pulled up in front of the workshop. The bookbinder Fernandez swept up to the door and opened it wide.

Greeting the author with deep respect,
he invited him in.

Under the Frenchman's arm was
a handwritten manuscript.

Although not so large, about the size of a prayer book, it was written on the most superlative paper. Watermarked with the author's crest, each folio had a lovely uneven deckle edge.

The writer explained to Señor Fernandez that the manuscript was very important. Indeed, he regarded it as his masterwork, and was planning to present it to the Pope.

Accordingly, the volume was to be bound in the rarest leather, the title embossed with the most expensive gold leaf.

For an hour or more, the author went over the details and the exact method of binding that was to be used. Price and time were, he insisted, no object.

The most superlative materials were to be sought out and used, and only the master craftsman himself was to work on the binding.

When Señor Fernandez enquired how long
he might be given to complete the task,
the writer shrugged.
'Take all the time you require,' he said.
'But remember that I am expecting the
best work of your life!'

The French author opened a briefcase, removed a purse filled with gold coins, and poured the currency onto my master's palm.

The two men shook hands.
A moment later, the wheels of the lacquered carriage turned, and the writer was gone.

As soon as he had left, my master collapsed onto a chair and thrust his head into his hands. 'Where will I get a piece of leather worthy of this manuscript?' he asked over and over.

I motioned at the swatches on display. 'None of them will do, you fool!' the bookbinder cried. 'How can you offer coal when we are in need of a diamond!'

A few days passed,
and then weeks,
and even months.

Señor Fernandez descended into a terrible depression. He began to drink heavily, and we feared he had forgotten about the French author's commission altogether.

Whenever an apprentice mentioned it, the
craftsman would fly into a rage and bawl at us.
'Without the right leather,' he declared,
'how can I begin?!'

Then, one chill morning in September,
Señor Fernandez was reading a letter from
a correspondent at his desk when, suddenly,
he leapt to his feet.

Waving the paper in the air, his face
gripped with mania, he yelled:
'*This* is the answer! *This* is the answer!'

The apprentices gathered round.
Taking the letter, I read aloud from
the bottom of the page:

'A new species of mammal has been seen for the first time in the Spice Islands. It has been named the "capilongo". A cross between a boar and a bird, it has the hands of a monkey and the intelligence of a human child. No one has yet managed to catch the capilongo alive.'

The veteran bookbinder instructed his apprentices to line up and to clear their minds. We did so, and he then asked for a volunteer – for a man sufficiently brave or foolhardy to go and capture the capilongo.

Only that creature's leather would do,
he insisted, for a masterwork
destined for the Pope.

No one volunteered.

One by one, the apprentices stepped back in trepidation and fear. After all, they were bookbinders, not explorers.

Unsure quite why, I leant forward, no more than an inch or two, but it was enough.

'I will do it,' I said in less than a whisper.
'I will go and capture the jungle beast
and bring back its hide.'

The next day, I set off.

I travelled first to Constantinople, and from there voyaged by sailing ship, dhow, and hollowed-out canoe, until I reached the pristine waters of the Spice Islands.

Never has an adventurer embarked
on a journey with less preparation
or know-how than I.

Until then, I was a raw page waiting
for a story of its own.

All I knew was that the capilongo was out there, somewhere, and that if I could hunt it, capture it, and skin it, then there would be a smile on the lips of an old bookbinder, a writer, and possibly the Pope as well.

The voyage was uncomfortable in the extreme. But, in my untested condition, I hardly knew the meaning of the word *discomfort*. Had I any inkling of what was to come, I would have savoured the weeks I spent upon turbulent seas.

The one meeting of interest was with a missionary who was drunk from one dawn to the next. He was accompanying a shipment of Bibles, printed in Cintra. He told me that they were destined for tattooed savages.

'Where are they, the savages?' I asked.
'Deep in the jungle,' came the assured reply.

After a great many deviations, the vessel docked at a ramshackle port. I descended the gangplank onto the quay, the name of a mythical creature filling my head and hovering on my tongue.

With no idea how to proceed, I followed
the bales of Bibles destined for savages.

There is no feeling quite so contrary as arriving in a foreign land with no grasp of language or etiquette. The heat was the first thing that hit me, dead straight between the eyes.

Unloaded by sweat-drenched stevedores,
the bales of Bibles were hauled in fits and starts
towards that terrible seething undergrowth.

And I followed them.

The missionary bought a bottle of home-made liquor, quaffed it down, and thanked God for protecting him.

'Pray to the Lord so that you, too, might be blessed,' he urged caustically. 'Neglect the Saviour, and the Angel of Death will be your shadow.'

Draining the bottle, he reeled about. 'The jungle...' he said after a long pause, rolling the word off his tongue as if it were the stone of a bitter olive. 'It will swallow you whole, devour you, then crush your bones to dust.'

We progressed on wagons and on mule carts, on hollowed-out logs and skiffs, until at last the precious cargo was unloaded on the banks of a great russet-brown river. It was all murky and warm, like bathwater left through a long, sultry afternoon, and it stank of both life and death.

The missionary drained another
bottle of liquor. Then another… and declared
that the Word of the Lord would be the
salvation of the savages.

Again, I enquired where they were,
the savage peoples of whom he spoke
so often and with such trepidation.

Raising a fist out, he pointed at the trees.
'They live on the Mountains of Medusa,'
he said.

With no other plan having presented itself,
I tagged along in the hope that the savages
would in turn lead me to the elusive capilongo.

A team of fresh porters was hired.
The Bibles and supplies having been laden
onto their backs, we set out from the river
and into the forest canopy.

After a few minutes of staggering under loads,
we found ourselves in a fearful realm of nature.

The towering trees reminded us of our frailty.
The creepers and the vines tripped us, the
chorus of unfamiliar sounds haunted
each wretched step.

The missionary kept the porters content
with a ration of dates in honey.
But it soon ran out.

When it did so, he resorted to a whip.
Any man who refused to pull his weight
was lashed to the bone.

Each night we slung hammocks,
squeezed water from oversized
tubular flowers, and we prayed.

The missionary prayed that the Bibles would reach the savages, and I prayed that I would find the capilongo, smite it, and return to my master with its skin.

The porters had never ventured into the undergrowth before. They spent their lives down at the river and said that only a madman would wish to trek towards the hinterland.

When I asked them about the Mountains of Medusa, they seemed to shake with fear.

Then, one morning, the missionary and I
awoke to find ourselves alone. The porters
had absconded, taking the supplies with them.
The only thing they left was the Bibles.

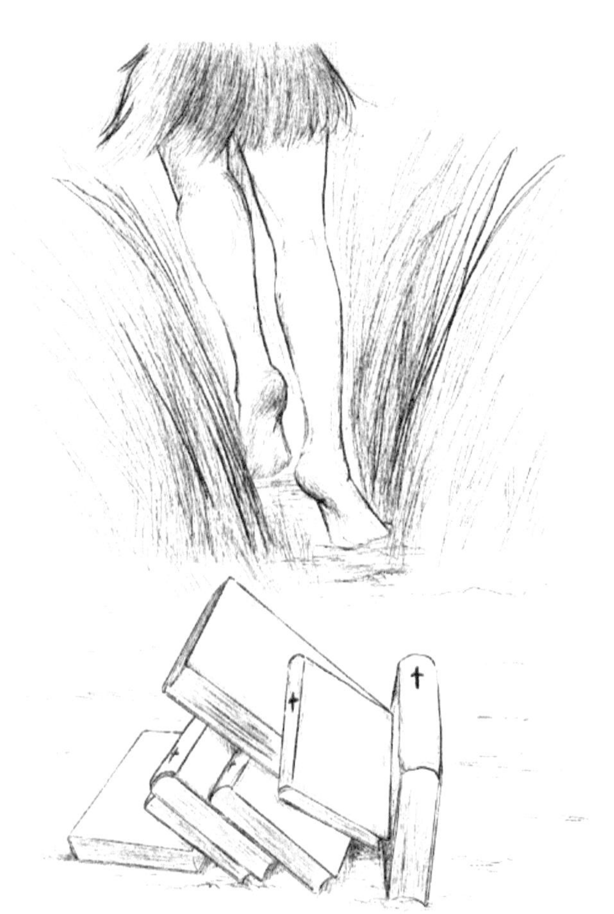

We called out,
our voices heard only by the trees.
'We can try and retrace our steps to the river,'
I said limply.

The missionary spat at the idea. Opening one of the boxes, he removed half a dozen of the Bibles. They were well bound in indigo buckram, silver lettering down the spine.

'The savages need the Word of the Lord,'
he said firmly, 'and so I will go on.'
'You will die,' I replied.

The missionary smiled at my remark. Smoothing a hand down over his grey beard, he said: 'The Lord is my protector and He is my guide.'

With that, he turned on his heel and moved boisterously into the undergrowth, clutching an armful of the holy books.

For a long time, I paused there in silence, unsure of what to do. There would have been safety in numbers, but the missionary was hell-bent on suicide.

Without food or equipment, he had less than no hope of survival, with or without the Word of the Lord.

Standing there, the jungle encroaching from all around, I was overcome with a vision.

In my mind's eye I glimpsed a great and unwieldy creature with the snout of a pig and the feathers of a bird. Poised erect on two feet, taller than a man, it appeared to have a very singular presence.

As I watched the hallucination, the creature – what I supposed to be the capilongo – opened a leather bag, removed a book, and began to read.

I blinked, and the vision was gone.

For seven days and nights I waited there at the same spot, the emerald canopy pressing ever closer, hunger gnawing at my ribs.

I survived by squeezing water from the tubular flowers and by eating the berries of the low shrubs that were common on the forest floor. I might have retraced my steps down to the river, but I had no idea in which direction it lay.

Something inside me was telling me to wait.
So I did.

And then, on the seventh night,
the vision came again.

This time, the capilongo was not reading
but smoking a pipe, staring into the
embers of a dying fire.

As I watched, he narrowed his eyes,
and he whispered:
'Dear apprentice, I know you are
watching me. And I am waiting for you.'

Then, as if answering my
unspoken question, he added:
'Follow the golden bird.'

At dawn the next day, I was woken by the shrill sound of a tiny bird, no larger than a hummingbird. It was hovering beside my face, as if hoping to gain my attention.

Rubbing my eyes, I saw that it wished for me to follow it. I jumped up and, before I knew it, I was running through the jungle in pursuit of the golden bird.

I chased and chased, the tangle of vines and
twisted branches hampering each footstep.
The little bird seemed to understand that
I was an unfamiliar visitor to its jungle.

Floundering about clumsily, I wished for wings to take to the air as the bird could. From time to time it would hover beside me, allowing me to catch my breath before hurrying on.

By dusk on the first day,
I reached a glade of empty ground.

Pinned out in the centre of it was the headless body of a man. Even before I had drawn near, I had guessed its identity, for all around it were torn pages – the Word of the Lord.

I buried the missionary under a pile
of flat-sided stones and read a passage
from Genesis over him.

I ought to have had fear, because his head was missing – chopped off, I imagined, by savages – savages surely more enlightened than him. Yet, for the first time since my departure from Toledo, I had hope.

Through the hours of three more days
I chased the golden bird, until the air
became cool and free from the insects
that plagued my waking hours.

While crouching on the banks of a little stream in rest, chewing a handful of berries, I fell back with shock.

Standing over me was the capilongo.

'Excuse me for startling you,'
he said in a polite voice.

I breathed in hard, choking in surprise.

The capilongo reached down and offered me his hand. It was soft, covered in chocolate-brown feathers.

'I saw you in a dream,' I said.
'And I saw you,' the curious creature replied,
'and I know why you have come.'

Glancing at the ground,
I mumbled the word ‘duty’.

'Before you kill me and take my skin,' said the capilongo, 'please do me the honour of dining with me. You see, I have very little chance to make intelligent conversation.'

I agreed readily.
After all, it was the least I could do.

The creature led me to a cave behind the stream. Gigantic, it was carpeted in scented moss and illuminated by shafts of natural light.

Arranged down the middle
was a long banquet table,
with two places laid at one end.

Welcoming me to his home,
the capilongo ushered me to the head
of the table and clapped his hands.

Nothing happened –
not for a moment, at least.

Then, slowly, an army of sloths slipped from the shadows, their long, curved arms laden with dishes and plates.

We dined on wild fruits, the seeds of which looked like cut diamonds, slivers of raw blue meat, and a kind of jelly that smelled of frogs. The sloth servants ferried one dish after another to the table.

I asked if there were savages living near.
The capilongo looked up sharply.

'There is a tribe up in the mountains,' he said, reaching for a segment of fruit. 'They live on the toasted, roasted brains of their vanquished foes. The skulls are stored beneath the ground in vats, pickled for months in the juice from the lowreeh tree.'

‘Do they hunt capilongos?’ I asked.
My host sniffed.
‘I am pleased to report that they do not,’
he said.

Before I could reply, the capilongo reached down and picked up a knife. An assassin's dagger of sorts, it had a sharp point and a long, straight shaft. He turned it carefully so that the blade was held in his fingers, the hilt pointing towards my chest.

‘Capilongos have two traditions,’
he said in a kindly tone. ‘The first is always
to assist a guest in anything they might require.
The second is to entertain an assassin before
he carries out his duty.

‘This knife is sharp enough to stab
me easily in the heart, or to slit my throat,
whichever you prefer. But before you
dispatch me, I would ask that you
permit me a small indulgence.’

Wondering what it was, I nodded.
'Yes, yes, of course.'

‘Would you mind me regaling you with
a story? Think of it as an entertainment,
a parting gift.’

I could hardly believe what I was hearing. But, delighted at having arrived at my quarry so easily, I accepted.

The capilongo clapped his hands and
the sloth servants cleared the plates.
When the serving dishes were gone,
an elderly sloth glided over to the table.

Between his upturned hands was held a salver, a bottle of aged jungle brandy balanced expertly upon it. Two glasses of the tawny liquid were poured.

The capilongo lit his pipe and his tale began.

But that, my dear friends, is another story.

*Finis*

*About the Author*

Descended from a long line of storytellers, writers, and savants, Tahir Shah is one of the most prolific authors of his generation. He has published more than sixty books in numerous genres, including travel, fiction, and fantasy, as well as tales for children.

Raised in the tradition of Eastern 'teaching stories', Shah is passionate about stories and storytelling. He regards the ability to learn from folklore as being in us all, what he calls a 'default setting of humankind'. As well as having written scores of books, Shah has made documentaries for National Geographic TV and The History Channel. He is the founder and CEO of the charity, The Scheherazade Foundation.

*About the Artist*

Beata Banach is an artist and illustrator from Lublin, Poland. Always fascinated with anything related to drawing and painting, she holds a master's degree in fine arts from the Maria Curie Skłodowska University in eastern Poland where she majored in traditional easel painting. Beata's main inspiration for her art is nature and travelling; she currently illustrates for writers from all over the world, specializing in children's books.

*Books By Tahir Shah*

*The Writer's Craft*

The Reason to Write

Workbook: Comprehensive, Volume I & II

Workbook: Fantasy, Volume I & II

Workbook: Fiction, Volume I & II

Workbook: Historical Fiction, Volume I & II

Workbook: Teaching Stories, Volume I & II

Workbook: Travel, Volume I & II

*Novels*

Jinn Hunter: Book One – The Prism

Jinn Hunter: Book Two – The Jinnslayer

Jinn Hunter: Book Three – The Perplexity

Hannibal Fogg and the Supreme Secret of Man

Casablanca Blues

Eye Spy

Godman

Paris Syndrome

Timbuctoo

Midas

Zigzagzone

*Nasrudin*

Travels With Nasrudin

The Misadventures of the Mystifying Nasrudin

The Peregrinations of the Perplexing Nasrudin

The Voyages and Vicissitudes of Nasrudin

Nasrudin in the Land of Fools

*Travel*

Trail of Feathers

Travels With Myself

Beyond the Devil's Teeth

In Search of King Solomon's Mines

House of the Tiger King

In Arabian Nights

The Caliph's House

Sorcerer's Apprentice

Journey Through Namibia

*Teaching Stories*

The Arabian Nights Adventures

Scorpion Soup

Tales Told to a Melon

The Afghan Notebook

Daydreams of an Octopus & Other Stories

The Caravanserai Stories

Ghoul Brothers

Hourglass

Imaginist

Jinn's Treasure

Jinnlore

Mellified Man

Skeleton Island

Wellspring

When the Sun Forgot to Rise

Outrunning the Reaper

The Cap of Invisibility

On Backgammon Time

The Wondrous Seed

The Paradise Tree
Mouse House
The Hoopoe's Flight
The Old Wind
A Treasury of Tales
The Tale of Double Six
The Forgotten Game
King of the Jinns
The Destiny Ring
Changing the World
Cat, Mouse
Frogland
Mittle-Mittle
Capilongo
The Princess of Zilzilam
The Singing Serpents
The Tale of the Rusty Nail
The Unicorn's Tear
The Clockmaker Who Travelled Through Time
The Fish's Dream
The Man Whose Arms Grew Branches
The Most Foolish of Men
The Shop That Sold Truth
Qwerty
Renaissance
The Man With the Tiger's Head
The Kingdom of Blink
The Wisdom of Celestine
Dream Soup
The Skeleton Factory
An Unexpected Gift

The Problem Exchange
The Pharaoh Code
The Monkey Puzzle Club
Liquid Time
Cat Dog, Dog Cat
Princess Pickle's Laugh

*Anthologies*
The Anthologies: Africa
The Anthologies: Ceremony
The Anthologies: Childhood
The Anthologies: City
The Anthologies: Danger
The Anthologies: East
The Anthologies: Expedition
The Anthologies: Frontier
The Anthologies: Hinterland
The Anthologies: India
The Anthologies: Jinns
The Anthologies: Jungle
The Anthologies: Magic
The Anthologies: Morocco
The Anthologies: Nasrudin
The Anthologies: People
The Anthologies: Quest
The Anthologies: South
The Anthologies: Taboo
The Anthologies: Teaching Stories
The Clockmaker's Box
The Tahir Shah Fiction Reader
The Tahir Shah Travel Reader

*Research*

Cultural Research

The Middle East Bedside Book

Three Essays

*Edited by*

Congress With a Crocodile

A Son of a Son, Volume I

A Son of a Son, Volume II

*Screenplays*

Casablanca Blues: The Screenplay

Timbuctoo: The Screenplay

## A REQUEST

If you enjoyed this book, please review it on your favourite online retailer or review website.

**Reviews are an author's best friend.**

To stay in touch with Tahir Shah, and to hear about his upcoming releases before anyone else, please sign up for his mailing list:

 http://tahirshah.com/newsletter

And to follow him on social media, please go to any of the following links:

 http://www.twitter.com/humanstew

 @tahirshah999

 http://www.facebook.com/TahirShahAuthor

 http://www.youtube.com/user/tahirshah999

 http://www.pinterest.com/tahirshah

 https://www.goodreads.com/tahirshahauthor

**http://www.tahirshah.com**

www.ingramcontent.com/pod-product-compliance
Lightning Source LLC
Chambersburg PA
CBHW030521310726
48979CB00010B/1759/J

*9781915876041*